The House that Jack Built

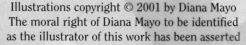

For Kelly, Joh and Guy – D. M.

Barefoot Books
37 West 17th Street
4th Floor East
New York, New York 10011

This book has been printed on 100% acid-free paper

This book was typeset in Clearface Regular 24pt
The illustrations were prepared in acrylics on hotpress watercolor paper

Graphic design by designsection, England
Color separation by Grafiscan, Italy
Printed and bound in Hong Kong by South China Printing Company (1988) Ltd.

1 3 5 7 9 8 6 4 2

U.S. Cataloging-in-Publication Data (Library of Congress Standards)

The house that Jack built / [illustrated by] Diana Mayo.
[24] p. : col. ill. ; 26 cm.
Summary: The classic children's rhyme enhanced with bold,
colorful artwork.
ISBN: 1-84148-251-X
1. Nursery rhymes. 2. Children's poetry. I. Mayo, Diana. II. Title.
398/.8 21 2001   AC   CIP

The House that Jack Built

Diana Mayo

Barefoot Books
better books for children

This is the house that Jack built.

This is the malt
That lay in the house
that Jack built.

This is the rat

That ate the malt

That lay in the house that Jack built.

This is the cat that chased the rat,

That ate the malt
That lay in the house that Jack built.

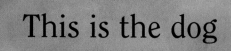

This is the dog

That worried the cat,

That chased the rat,

That ate the malt

That lay in the house that Jack built.

This is the cow with the crumpled horn,

That tossed the dog,

That worried the cat,

That chased the rat,

That ate the malt

That lay in the house that Jack built.

This is the maiden all forlorn,

That milked the
cow with the
crumpled horn,

That tossed the dog,

That worried the cat,

That chased the rat,

That ate the malt

That lay in the house that Jack built.

This is the man all tattered and torn,

That kissed the maiden all forlorn,

That milked the cow with the crumpled horn,

That tossed the dog,

That worried the cat,

That chased the rat,

That ate the malt

That lay in the house that Jack built.

This is the priest all shaven and shorn,

That married the man all tattered and torn,

That kissed the maiden all forlorn,

That milked the cow with the crumpled horn,

That tossed the dog,

That worried the cat,

That chased the rat,

That ate the malt

That lay in the house that Jack built.

This is the cock that crowed in the morn,

That waked the priest all
shaven and shorn,

That married the man
all tattered and torn,

That kissed the maiden all forlorn,

That milked the cow with the
crumpled horn,

That tossed the dog,

That worried the cat,

That chased the rat,

That ate the malt

That lay in the house that Jack built.

This is the farmer sowing his corn,

That kept the cock that crowed in the morn,

That waked the priest all shaven and shorn,

That married the man all tattered and torn,
That kissed the maiden all forlorn,

That tossed the dog,

That milked the cow
with the crumpled horn,

That worried the cat,

That chased the rat,

That ate the malt

That lay in the house that Jack built.

Barefoot Books
better books for children

At Barefoot Books, we celebrate art and story with books that open
the hearts and minds of children from all walks of life, inspiring them to read
deeper, search further, and explore their own creative gifts. Taking our
inspiration from many different cultures, we focus on themes that encourage
independence of spirit, enthusiasm for learning, and acceptance of other
traditions. Thoughtfully prepared by writers, artists and storytellers from
all over the world, our products combine the best of the present with the best
of the past to educate our children as the caretakers of tomorrow.
www.barefootbooks.com